Who Says?

Note

Once a reader can recognize and identify the 16 words used to tell this story, he or she will be able to read successfully the entire book. These 16 words are repeated throughout the story, so that young readers will be able to easily recognize the words and understand their meaning.

The 16 words used in this book are:

bark	croak	horse	quack
chicken	dog	neigh	says
cluck	duck	of	the
course	frog	owl	who

Library of Congress Cataloging-in-Publication Data
Hall, Kirsten.
    Who says?/by Kirsten Hall & Jessica Flaxman; illustrated by
Wayne Becker.
        p.   cm.—(My first reader)
    Summary: Singing before a musical conductor, animals from chicken
to owl reveal their own special sounds.
        Previously published by Grolier.
        ISBN 0-516-05362-0
        (1. Animal sounds—Fiction. 2. Singing—Fiction. 3. Stories in
rhyme.) I. Flaxman, Jessica. II. Becker, Wayne, ill. III. Title.
IV. Series
PZ8.3.H146Wh 1990
(E)—dc20
                                            90-1413
                                            CIP
                                            AC

Who Says?

Written by Kirsten Hall and Jessica Flaxman
Illustrated by Wayne Becker

 CHILDRENS PRESS ®
CHICAGO

Text © 1990 Nancy Hall, Inc. Illustrations © Wayne Becker.
All rights reserved. Published by Childrens Press®, Inc.
Printed in the United States of America. Published simultaneously in Canada.
Developed by Nancy Hall, Inc. Designed by Antler & Baldwin Design Group.

1 2 3 4 5 6 7 8 9 10 R 99 98 97 96 95 94 93 92 91 90

Cluck says the chicken.

Cluck, cluck, cluck.

9

Who says quack?

11

Of course, the duck!

13

Bark, bark, bark.

Bark says the dog.

Who says croak?

19

Croak says the frog.

Neigh, neigh, neigh.

Neigh says the horse.

25

Who says who?

The owl, of course!